SWEET DAYS OF DISCIPLINE

"Startling and original...so disturbing and so haunting."
—Cathleen Schine, *The New York Review of Books*

"Nothing rivals its intensity."
—*The Los Angeles Times Book Review*

"Spare, bleak, haunting...quite beautiful...a rich and affecting book, animated by a disciplined austerity, its terse beauties falling on the reader like a chaste, gray rain."
—*The New Republic*

"Small-scale, intense, and impeccably focused."
—*The New Yorker*

"I can't tell you how strongly it moved me and filled me with admiration. I've never read anything like it....The beauty of such darkness and the prose of the book are remarkable."
—John Hawkes

"How a novel could be so chilly and so passionate at the same time is a puzzle, but that icy-hot quality is only one of the distinctions of *Sweet Days of Discipline*."
—April Bernard, *New York Newsday*

"Delicately imbued with an unbalanced, maniacal quality and with nuances of emotion woven and unravelled simultaneously. Fleur Jaeggy has an extraordinary ability to create character and atmosphere." —*World Literature Today*

"She has the enviable first glance for people and things, she harbors a mixture of distracted levity and authoritative wisdom." —Ingeborg Bachmann

Sweet Days of Discipline

by FLEUR JAEGGY

Translated by TIM PARKS

A NEW DIRECTIONS BOOK

Published by arrangement with William Heinemann Ltd., London.
Originally published in Italy as *I beati anni del castigo* (Adelphi Edizioni).

Manufactured in the United States of America
New Directions Books are printed on acid-free paper
First published as New Directions Original Paperbook 758 in 1993

Library of Congress Cataloging-in-Publication Data
Jaeggy, Fleur.
[Beati anni del castigo. English]
Sweet days of discipline / Fleur Jaeggy ; translated by Tim Parks.
p. cm. — (New Directions paperbook ; 758)
ISBN 0-8112-1235-1
I. Title.
PQ4870.A4B4313 1993 93-9196
853'.914—dc20 CIP

10 9 8 7 6 5 4

New Directions Books are published for James Laughlin
by New Directions Publishing Corporation
80 Eighth Avenue, New York 10011

At fourteen I was a boarder in a school in the Appenzell. This was the area where Robert Walser used to take his many walks when he was in the mental hospital in Herisau, not far from our college. He died in the snow. Photographs show his footprints and the position of his body in the snow. We didn't know the writer. And nor did our literature teacher. Sometimes I think it might be nice to die like that, after a walk, to let yourself drop into a natural grave in the snows of the Appenzell, after almost thirty years of mental hospital, in Herisau. It really is a shame we didn't know of Walser's existence, we would have picked a flower for him. Even Kant, shortly before his death, was moved when a woman he didn't know offered him a rose. You can't help but take walks in the Appenzell. If you look at the small white-framed windows and the busy, fiery flowers on the sills, you get this sense of tropical stagnation, a thwarted luxuriance, you have the feeling that inside something serenely gloomy and a little sick is going on. It's an Arcadia of sickness. Inside, it seems, in the brightness in there, is the peace and perfection of death, a rejoicing of whitewash and flowers. Outside the windows, the landscape beckons; it isn't a mirage, it's a *Zwang*, as we used to say in school, a duty.

I was studying French, German and general culture. I wasn't studying at all. The only thing I remember of French literature is Baudelaire. Every morning I got up at five to go out and walk. I climbed high up the hill and saw a strip of water on the other side, down at the bottom. Lake Constance. I looked at the horizon, and at the lake; I didn't realise as yet that another school awaited me by that lake. I ate an apple and walked. I was looking for solitude, and perhaps the absolute. But I envied the world.

It happened one day at lunch. We had all sat down. A girl arrived, a new one. She was fifteen, she had hair straight and shiny as blades and stern staring shadowy eyes. Her nose was aquiline, her teeth when she laughed, and she didn't often laugh, were sharp. She had a fine, high forehead, the kind of forehead that makes thought tangible, a forehead past generations had endowed with talent, intelligence and charm. She spoke to no one. Her looks were those of an idol, disdainful. Perhaps that was why I wanted to conquer her. She had no humanity. She even seemed repulsed by us all. The first thing I thought was: she had been further than I had. When we rose from the table, I went up to her and said: '*Bonjour.*' Her *Bonjour* was brusque. I introduced myself, name and surname, like a recruit, and when she had told me hers it seemed the conversation was over. She left me there in the dining hall, amongst the other chattering girls. A Spanish girl told me something in an excited voice, but I paid no attention. I heard a clamour of different languages. That whole day the new arrival didn't show her face, but in the evening she appeared punctually for dinner, tall behind her chair. Standing still, it was as if she were veiled. At a nod from the headmistress we all sat down and after a few moments' silence everyone was talking again. The following day it was she greeted me first.

In our lives at school, each of us, if we had a little vanity, would establish a façade, a kind of double life, affect a way of speaking, walking, looking. When I saw her writing I couldn't believe it. We almost all had the same kind of handwriting, uncertain, childish, with round, wide 'o's. Hers was completely affected. (Twenty years later I saw something similar in a dedication Pierre Jean Jouve had written on a copy of *Kyrie.*) Of course I pretended not to be surprised, I barely glanced at it. But secretly I practised. And I still write like Frédérique today, and people tell me I have beautiful, interesting handwriting. They don't know how hard I worked at it. In those days I didn't work at all, and I never worked at school, because I didn't want to. I cut out reproductions of the German expressionists and crime stories from the papers and pasted them in an exercise book. I led her to believe I was interested in art. As a result Frédérique granted me the honour of accompanying her along the corridors and on her walks. At school – though I think it goes without saying – she was top in everything. She already knew everything, from the generations that came before her. She had something the others didn't have; all I could do was justify her talent as a gift passed on from the dead. You only had to hear her reciting the French poets in class to realise that they had come down to her, were reincarnated in her. We, perhaps, were still innocent. And perhaps innocence has something crude, pedantic and affected about it, as if we were all dressed in plus fours and long socks.

We came from all over the world, lots of Americans and Dutch. One girl was coloured, as they say today, a little black girl, curly-haired, a doll for us to admire in the Appenzell. She had arrived one day with her father. He was President of an African state. One girl of every nationality was chosen to form a fan shape at the entrance to the Bausler Institut. There was a redhead, a Belgian, a Swedish blonde, the Italian girl, the girl from Boston. They all cheered the President, lined up with their flags in their hands, and they truly did represent the world. I was in the third row, the last, next to Frédérique, the hood of my duffel coat pulled over my head. In front – and if the President had had a bow, his arrow would have pierced her heart – stood the headmistress of the school, Frau Hofstetter, tall, heavily built, very dignified, a smile buried in her fat cheeks. Next to her was her husband, Herr Hofstetter, a thin, small, shy man. They raised the Swiss flag. The little black girl took the leading position in the formation. It was cold. She was wearing a dark-blue, bell-shaped coat, a lighter-blue velvet collar. I must confess that the black President cut a good figure at the Bausler Institut. The African head of state trusted the Hofstetter family. There were one or two Swiss girls who weren't impressed by the pomp with which the President had been received. They said all fathers should be treated as equals. There are always a few subversives tucked away in a boarding school. The first signs of their political thinking emerge, or of what you might call a general vision of the whole. Frédérique had a Swiss flag in her hand and looked as though she were holding a pole. The youngest girl curtsied and offered a bunch of wild flowers. I don't remember if the black girl ever managed to make friends with anybody. We often saw the headmistress holding her hand and taking her for walks. Yes, Frau Hofstetter in person. Maybe she was afraid we would eat the girl. Or that she wouldn't stay pure. She never played tennis.

Frédérique became more and more distant every day. Sometimes I would go to see her in her room. I slept in another house, she was with the older girls. Although there were only a few months between us, I had to stay with the younger girls. I shared my room with a German whose name I've forgotten, she was so uninteresting. She gave me a book on the German expressionists. Frédérique's cupboard was incredibly tidy, I didn't know how to fold pullovers so that not so much as a centimetre was out of place and I had a low mark for tidiness. I learnt from her. Sleeping in separate houses it was as if there were a generation between us. One day I found a little love note in my pigeon hole, it was from a ten-year-old who begged me to let her become my favourite, to make a pair. Impulsively I answered with an unfriendly no, and I still regret it today. I regretted it then too, immediately, no sooner than I'd told her that I had no use for a sister, that I wasn't interested in looking after a little favourite. I was getting to be unpleasant because Frédérique was eluding me and I had to conquer her, because it would be too humiliating to lose. I only took a look at the younger girl when it was too late and I had already offended her. She was really pretty, very attractive, and I had lost a slave, without getting any pleasure out of it.

The younger girl never spoke to me again from that day on, nor even said hello. As you see, I had yet to learn the art of compromise, I still thought that to get something you had to go straight for your goal, whereas it is only distractions, uncertainty, distance that bring us closer to our targets, and then it is the target which strikes us. Yet I did have a strategy with Frédérique. I had a reasonable amount of experience of boarding school life. I'd been a boarder since I was eight years old. And it's in the dormitories that you get to know your fellow boarders, by the washbasins, at break time. My first boarding school bed was surrounded by white curtains, and covered with a white piqué bedspread. Even the dresser was white. A pretend room, followed by twelve others. A sort of chaste promiscuity. You could hear the sighs. My room-mate in the Bausler Institut was a German, well-behaved and mean the way stupid girls often can be. In bright white underwear her body was quite attractive, shapely almost, but if by accident I were to touch her I had a feeling of repugnance. Maybe that's why I got up so early in the morning for my walks. By eleven, during the lessons, I would start feeling sleepy. I looked over to the window, and the window returned my expression and had me dozing off.

Frédérique and I not only slept in different houses at night, we were also in different classrooms during the day. We didn't sit close to each other at table, but I could see her. And at last she began to look at me. Maybe I was interesting too. I liked German expressionism and the thought of the life, the crimes I hadn't yet experienced. I told her that at ten I had insulted a mother superior by calling her a cow. What a simple word, I was ashamed of my simplicity when I told her about it. I was expelled from the convent school. 'Beg pardon,' they said. I wouldn't. Frédérique laughed. She was kind enough to ask me why I'd done it. And gradually I began to talk about myself at eight years old. At the time I used to play football with the boys, then they sent me to that dismal college. At the end of a dismal corridor was a chapel. To the left a door. Inside, a mother superior, ethereal, delicate, who took me under her wing. She caressed me with her slender, soft hands, she sat next to me as if I were a friend. One day she disappeared. In her place arrived a buxom Swiss from Canton Uri. It's common knowledge that a new leader will hate the predecessors' favourites. A boarding school is like a harem.

Frédérique told me I was an aesthete. It was a new word for me, but it immediately made sense. Her handwriting was an aesthete's handwriting, that much I appreciated. Likewise her scorn for everything was an aesthete's scorn. Frédérique hid her scorn behind obedience and discipline; she was respectful. I hadn't as yet learnt to dissemble. I was respectful with the headmistress, Frau Hofstetter, because I was afraid of her. I was ready to curtsey to her. Frédérique never needed to curtsey, because her way of respecting others instilled respect. And I noticed this. Once, perhaps to distract myself from my pursuit of Frédérique, I accepted a date with a boy from a nearby boarding school, the Rosenberg. It was a short date. They saw me. Frau Hofstetter called me to her office. She was broad as a cupboard in a blue tailleur, white blouse, a brooch. She threatened me. I told her he was just a relative. It was true, in fact his mother had written to Frau Hofstetter on purpose to tell her to be careful that I didn't go to see him. I pretended to cry. She was touched. Where had all the strength I'd had at eight gone, the confidence, the self-control? At eight I hadn't given a moment's thought to any of the other girls. They were all the same, all detestable and mean. Even now, I can't bring myself to say I was in love with Frédérique, it's such an easy thing to say.

That day I was afraid they would throw me out. One morning, breakfasts were delicious, I dunked my bread in my coffee. Having slapped my dunking hand, the headmistress made me stand up. At eight I would have picked up my cup and tossed it in her face. Who gave her the right to insult me? Frédérique ate with her elbows pressed against her bust. Never did an elbow of Frédérique's touch the table. Did she scorn her food too? She was so perfect. When we went for walks together, every day now, the two of us alone, sometimes she would walk in front of me and I would watch her. Everything about her was right, harmonious. Sometimes she put her hand on my shoulder and it was as though it must stay like that forever, through the woods, the mountains, the paths, *une amitié amoureuse*, as the French say. She said something about a man. I had nothing to say on the subject, only my relative. And a governess. But it wasn't the same thing. A governess, a nun, a school friend are all of a kind. Frédérique spoke of a man as of a completed parabola. In the evening when I went back to my room with the German girl, I thought it over. Of course we are experts when it comes to women, we who have spent our best years in boarding schools. And when we get out, since the world is divided in two, male and female, we'll get to know the male side as well. But will it ever have the same intensity? Will conquering men, I wondered, be as difficult as conquering Frédérique?

Despite the daily walks with Frédérique, the confidences, the tenderness, I felt I hadn't conquered her yet. My term of comparison for what I was doing was force. I must conquer her, she must admire me. Frédérique did not grant her company to anyone, and sometimes she preferred to be alone rather than with me. And I would get bored. I didn't read, I looked at myself in the mirror, brushed my hair, a hundred brush strokes, I pretended to love nature. Frédérique, I'd noticed, did not look at herself in the mirror. How enthusiastically I talked to her about trees, mountains, silence and literature. Life was dragging on a bit for me. I'd been seven years in boarding schools already and there was more to come. When you're in boarding school you imagine how grand and fine the world is, and when you leave you'd sometimes like to hear the sound of the school bell again.

It's strange that whenever I went to college there was always a shortage of men round about. Either they were old, or mad, or caretakers. In the Appenzell I recall some ancient men, cripples, a cake shop and a fountain. If you wanted a bit of city life you went to the cake shop; there was never anybody there, but an old man might pass by along the road. For a long time I thought that those of us who had been in boarding school, like Frédérique and myself, would remember it all one day when we were old and disappointed and would be able to live on nothing. The bell rings, we get up. The bell rings again, we go to bed. We retire to our rooms; we saw life pass by beneath our windows, observed it in books and on our walks, watched the seasons change. It was always a reflection, a reflection that seemed to freeze on our windowsills. And perhaps now and then we saw a tall marbly figure stand out stark before us: it is Frédérique passing through our lives and maybe we'd like to go back, but we don't need anything, anymore. We imagined the world. What else can we imagine now if not our own deaths? The bell rings and it's all over.

But to return to our little story: Frédérique would describe the colours of the leaves to me, I remember our conversations as always being surrounded by freshness. The French literature teacher admired her, thought of her as a Brontë, perhaps. And detested me. She wanted it to be her taking the walks with Frédérique. She was an ugly woman, she didn't know about anything apart from French literature, to which she was devoted. When she spoke, I yawned. As I've already said, life was really dragging along slowly for me. Literature for its own sake didn't amuse me; the important thing was to prepare for my conversations with Frédérique. I had read a few lines of Novalis about suicide and perfection.

'But what's wrong with you?' 'What are you thinking about?' she asked me. At last she had asked me what I was thinking about. A point in my favour. There was only one thing I was thinking about: getting out into the world. And I would never admit it. Nothing, I answered Frédérique. I'm not thinking about anything. Sometimes, when we were talking together, I thought about her, about her beauty, her intelligence, something perfect there was about her. Years and years have passed and I can still see her face, a face I have looked for in other women and never found. She was entire unto herself. Something dangerous. I never had the straightforwardness to tell her, nor to confess my admiration, since from the very first day I always felt, despite a certain inferiority on my part in comparison with her, that before becoming close we would have to go through certain phases. Like in a battle. And I had to conquer her. Everything was so lofty and tense, words, tone and manner were weighed up, it took a certain mental effort. I wonder what would have happened if, after a few weeks, instead of talking we had begun to put our arms round each other. It would have been unthinkable. We never held hands. We would have thought it ridiculous. You saw little girls holding hands along the paths, laughing, playing girlfriends, playing lovers. With us there was a kind of fanaticism that prevented any physical expression.

The French mistress looked like a sad man, especially in the light, near the window, behind the teacher's desk. She asked me questions. I didn't answer. She had short, grey wavy hair, hands like a priest's, pressed together. Behind her austere gaze it was as if she were trying to beg almost, there was a never-to-be-satisfied supplication, a purity even, the purity of the loser, a mixture of fleeting desperation and stubbornness. They hang on, this kind.

They teach right to the end, on their deathbeds. They read a penultimate poem. She was still asking me questions, getting to her feet now. Did she want to beat me? I was vacuous, I was suffering from a sort of loss of will, as often happened towards midday. It had been seven hours since my morning walk. Seven hours is almost as long as a worker works, and they want to do less. She despises me. She must be asking herself why on earth Frédérique spends time with me, I can sense it in her expression. Maybe she understood. I couldn't read a book. In the bookcase, my section was empty. I leafed through Frédérique's books, but if anything needed real concentration I didn't have the energy. As for what might be called spiritual energy, Frédérique took up a great deal. When she talked to me about literature, I was really interested, and I had to be up on a par with her reflections, but even when she talked to me there were moments when I wasn't there.

Frédérique was beginning to look at me. I felt the weight of her eyes on my body. It was like a punch in the back sometimes, and I would turn. Sometimes, at table, I sensed her gaze on me, and then I held myself straighter and ate with the most refined manners, so that I hardly ate at all. But at breakfast, even if she was watching me, I helped myself to two or three slices of bread and butter and marmalade. And I have to admit that I thought of nothing but breakfast. When I dunked my bread in my coffee that time it was out of sheer greed, without thinking. I seem to remember Frédérique smiled, out of indulgence I suppose. Now she was asking me to spend time with her, and she kept her eye on me from a distance.

From the first day I saw her I wanted to be with her, and being with her really meant taking on her mind, becoming accomplices, disdaining all the others. Like blood brothers in a way, or sisters. And that from the very first day, from the moment she came late into the dining hall. Or I had to submit to a rite that she was celebrating. One day she told me that she had noticed me immediately, but she only said it to please me, even if she never said anything just to please. She may once have said that I was beautiful. Clearly I wasn't as elegant as she was. She wore grey skirts, loose blouses, grey, dark-blue or powder-blue pullovers, all loose. I had a lot of tight pullovers and wide skirts with very tight waists. I pulled the waist as tight as possible with broad belts, as almost everybody else did. And that is not elegance. Her loose pullovers hung over her body, hiding it, just letting you glimpse an adolescent figure, narrow hips, flat stomach.

One winter afternoon – we were sitting on the stairs – Frédérique took my hands and said: 'You've got an old woman's hands.' Hers were cold. She looked at the backs of my hands: you could count the veins and the bones. She turned them over: they were shrivelled up. I can hardly describe how proud I was to hear what for me was a compliment. That day, on the stairs, I knew she was attracted to me. They really were an old woman's hands, they were bony. Frédérique's hands were broad, thick, square, like a boy's. Both of us wore signet rings on our little fingers. You might imagine that we found physical pleasure in touching each other like this. As she touched my hand and I felt hers, cold, our contact was so anatomical that the thought of flesh or sensuality eluded us. That winter I bought myself a loose pullover and hid my body. My old woman's hands were all the more obvious.

Frédérique was always polite with everybody, she never let her moods get the better of her, she was never irritable. In this I couldn't copy her. On the contrary, there were some rare occasions when I wanted to give my room-mate a good beating. She was submissive, she always said I was right. She had dimples. And she never forgot to show them. A little snub nose. I wanted to wring her neck. She stretched out on her bed like a slave in a harem, half naked, this German girl.

They made us recite François Coppée. I am disturbed as I realise only today that Frédérique's initials were the same as the writer's. '*J'étais à ma fenêtre et je pensais à vous devant le ciel d'été.*' That was how my part began. '*Un rossignol chantait et ses notes perlées montaient éperdument aux voûtes étoilées.*' The teacher was a nun, she taught us how to recite in time to the piano.

Frédérique's surname means 'story'. And, since her name is a story, I'll let myself imagine that it's her dictating this story, or writing it, laughing in her caustic way. I also have an inexplicable premonition that the story has already been written. Is finished. Like our lives.

On Sankt Nikolaus day we spent a whole afternoon

out of school. It was snowing. We were mute. We went into the cake shop in Teufen. The village seemed rapt, sleepy. I knew that Fédérique had, or had had, a relationship with a man. It went on snowing, the flakes hanging still at the windows. Frédérique told me she would be taking a trip with him, at Christmas. I watched the snowflakes, intrigued, Frédérique spoke softly. I knew about her relationship and I certainly did not wish her an idyllic time. And I told her so, taking a pastry. Wouldn't she have another pastry? Another cup of tea. I didn't want confidences, or confessions. I had the impression there was something tragic in her love; she looked stubborn, determined. For a moment it occurred to me there was no man. I took another pastry. The snowflakes hung still. It crossed my mind that Frédérique was inventing another life for herself. Fleetingly, as she was speaking, I thought I saw a strange light in her eyes, like the snowflakes, mad and pointless, hanging still in the air. I was afraid, I wanted to tell her to save herself, but I didn't know from what. My thoughts were suspended halfway, I had the impression of danger, the danger of experiencing something which doesn't exist. Then everything was relaxed again, that glimmer of disorder faded away. Frédérique repeated that they would be going to Andalusia, they'd been there before. She asked me if I'd ever been to Spain. No, never. I'd been all over Switzerland, by train, because my father liked trains and changing trains, trains in the mountains. Had she ever been to Rigi? No, never. I mentioned the names of a few other mountains. Gornergrat, Jungfrau, the Bernina train. No.

Frédérique spoke about her travels as if talking about someone else. In the cake shop in Teufen it began to grow dark, as if even the snow were a curtain of dark. Outside the winter night. Outside, the freezing air escorted us home. Our home is the school.

Every evening my room-mate and I stood by the wash-basins. Once I had been friendly with her, her comb would drop and immediately I would bend down to pick it up. She combed her hair before going to bed as if she were going to a dance. And maybe she did go, in her sleep. Showing off her dimples to everyone. One canine protruded from her gums. She had a pink taffeta dress she took care not to crumple. Sometimes I was so sure she was going dancing I would see her pink dress over her chair at the foot of her bed where she had folded her little pile of underwear. Only on special occasions was there likely to be a room inspection. It would take place in the morning; you had to open all the cupboards; our little piles of folded underwear and pullovers must have looked like a great wall. Like the orientals, we were supposed to know the art of folding our things. Some time ago I went to see a Noh theatre company. At the end of the show I went backstage to say hello to an actor. He was packing his suitcase, or rather his bundle. He folded his clothes exactly the way we used to fold them in our cupboards. With the same discipline and a sort of submission toward the different materials. If I had agreed to become the protector of the little girl who had written me the note and left it in my pigeon hole, she would have kept things tidy for me. She would have considered it an honour to fold my pullovers. We were fetishists.

If I had given Marion – that was what the younger girl was called – a flower, she would have pressed it in a text book, it would have had to last forever. Of course it's quite common to buy an old book and find petals between the pages, petals that crumble to dust as soon as you touch them. Sick petals. Grave flowers. Her love for me dried up in an instant, didn't even leave any dust, she never spoke to me again. I tore up Marion's affectionate note at once, just as I at once tore up the rare letters from my mother or father. My room-mate kept everything in an inlaid wooden box, a German box.

She re-read her letters stretched lazily on her bed. German smells rose from the box, and they can't have been faint either, she was so avid to breathe in their essence. There was a gilded lock too, a tiny key. She would open the hideous thing with votive hands, the German girl.

I hardly got any letters. They were handed out at mealtimes. It wasn't nice not to get much post. So I began to write to my father, mindless letters saying nothing. I hoped he was well, I was well. He answered at once, sticking *Pro Juventute* stamps on the envelopes. He asked me why on earth I wrote to him so often. Both his letters and mine were short. Every month a banknote would be enclosed, my *argent de poche*. I wrote to him because I knew he was the only person who did as I asked, even though it was my mother who was legally in charge of me and it was to her decisions I had to submit. She sent her orders from Brasil. I had to have a German room-mate because I had to speak German. And I spoke to the German, she gave me presents, chocolates she was always eating, American chewing gum, and art books. In German. With German reproductions. Blaue Reiter. Even her underwear was German. And yet I can't find her name in the pigeon holes of my mind; girls lost in my memory. Who was she? She was such a non-entity for me, and yet I do remember her face and body. Perhaps, thanks to some malign trick, those we didn't pay any attention to rise up again. Their features are more deeply impressed on us than those we did give time to. Our minds are a series of graves in a wall. Our non-entities are all there when the register is called, gluttonous creatures; sometimes they fly up like vultures to hide the faces of those we loved. A multitude of faces dwell in the graves, a rich pasturage. While I write, the German girl is sketching out, as in a police station, her own particulars. What is her name? Her name is lost.

But it's not enough to forget a name to have forgotten the person. She's all there, in her grave in the wall.

It was clear I would have to spend the best years of my life in boarding school. From eight to seventeen. Previously they'd left me with an elderly lady, a grandmother. One day she decided she couldn't put up with me any more, she said I was a savage. And yet I resembled nothing so much as her portrait hanging in the dining room. That's why she wanted me out of her sight. Now I look more and more like her. She too is in one of the graves. With her indigo eyes. Thanks to her I went to a lot of boarding schools, got to know headmistresses, reverend mothers, mother superiors and *Mères préfètes*, but none of them had the authority my grandmother had. I always felt I could fool them, that their power was temporary, even if I did kiss their hands.

That happened in Italy, in a school run by French nuns, where, as usual, I was a boarder. Every evening, before going to bed, in dormitories as always, I would climb a narrow staircase with my companions. At the top, *Mère préfète* was waiting. Every evening she held out her hand under the dimmest possible lightbulb in the glimmer of the narrow stairs, before you went through into the night-time glow of the dormitories. Queuing up, we kissed her hand one by one. Then to the washbasins, then to bed, in the becalmed dormitories. The sheets felt stiff. Outside, if the moon and stars were up, lay a visionary desert.

They had taught us to curtsey, if I'm not mistaken, in four stages when in the presence of the reverend mother superior. I don't remember how the reverend *Mère préfète's* skin tasted, but I made that gesture of submission in exemplarily automatic fashion; I found it natural and I liked to stop and take in the whole scene with my companions queueing behind. Though holding her hand between thumb and index finger, my lips did not touch the skin; a sort of repugnance at our shared carnality crept over me.

The *Mère préfète's* eyes were blue as alpine lakes at dawn, childish and venomous. She was so much a *fin de race* that her eyelids had turned to white lead; generations of supplicants must have kissed the hands of her forebears, before the guillotine. She had an oriental look to her, her forehead was covered with a veil, and veils are becoming on women, even old women. They confer majesty and mystery. And treachery. There was something soft about her body, something *faisandé*. The imminence of her return to dust, to ashes, and her imperious cream-coloured robes, conspired with the stiffness natural to her status to make her look like some great dame of sepulchres. Her voice was querulous sometimes, and extremely young, the way you might imagine the voices of eunuchs.

There, with the French nuns, I beheld class distinctions in all their sharpness. There were the dark-robed nuns, they were the humblest, the ones with no dowry, the poor who had to do the heavy jobs for the others. We addressed them as 'sister', and we could show disdain if we so desired. The reverend mothers treated them with condescension and bright buttery smiles. And in that school we all knew which of us were poor or orphans. There was one girl who didn't pay the fees, and she did favours and little kindnesses for the *Mère préfète*. And maybe she spied. We were kind to her, she came from a family that had come down in the world, her eyes were silky blue and yellow. She was blonde and she came from the south; but a bothersome flibbertigibbet, because she was a spy. A spy, we supposed, out of necessity. We could have given her much more than the very reverend mothers did, but she was naturally inclined to be submissive to authority. Some people are born like that. We tried to win her over, but she wasn't interested. She should have been taller, her calves were close to her ankles, there was no lift to her figure. Seated she was very pretty, her complexion and the colour of her hair suited her small slightly rough pottery face. She was an older pupil, kept out of charity. She was over eighteen, and that was sad. She practised her vocation – to us it seemed a profession – of being poor very well.

She attached a value to her poverty, the way others might to their extravagance. She was truly possessed by her indigent state, all she had was herself, but it was more than enough, since the aromas of servitude bubbled up from her constantly, a natural predisposition. How small and slippery her feet were when she went quick as quick up and down the corridor, and how well she knew how to disappear when the reverend mother called her, barely whispering her name. Reverend mothers always speak very softly. And how she would genuflect sideways in the chapel! Her big eyes were well suited to contemplating the crucifix. If she hadn't been an informer, we would have believed, generously, in her magnanimous devotion and obedience.

At the Bausler Institut you don't kiss the headmistress's hand. It's Frau Hofstetter who sometimes pretends to kiss your cheeks. She touches your cheek with her own and, even though this gesture has nothing to do with kissing, it is monstrous all the same. I don't know how the little black girl can put up with it. She gets real kisses, we've seen. And she doesn't give the slightest impression of being in need of affection, the black girl. Her expression is changing. It no longer looks like a doll's, it is losing that depth toys have, that impassive, fatuous rigidity, that stupor of good little children.

Almost all of us have been lured into a state of stupor. Especially one small group of older girls. In the first term they were lazy, slothful and could barely speak in German, they had already been together in Kiruna or somewhere, they were almost married already, too adult for the Bausler. In boarding schools, or at least the ones where I went, a sort of senile childhood was protracted almost to insanity. We knew why those big girls with their exhausted vivacity sat down throughout recreation periods, as though waiting, whispering to each other and looking after their complexions. They were the clique of the experienced; they had already given themselves to the world, or at least so they would have had us believe. The first round was over and the next rounds buzzed like halos round their golden heads. They were the old ones.

'Couldn't you let me change room? I'd like to sleep in the older girls' house.' Frau Hofstetter had greeted me kindly, asking me if I would be going for a walk with my friend Frédérique again today. Her voice seemed to dwell on the word, friend. So, in the eyes of the authorities, Frédérique and I were a pair. 'We are happy that you've found a friend. But you won't be changing room. That was settled at the beginning of the year. Your mother writes to us from Brasil, and she, like us, is satisfied with your room-mate.' Satisfactions have to stagnate. Her ruined eyes, her face powder and blue tailleur with brooch came up close. She caressed my head with a vague gesture. In some women, the facial skin cracks with using make up. '*Danke, Frau Hofstetter.*' You must always say thank you, even when they have refused you something. Part of your education is learning how to thank with a smile. An awful smile. There is a mortuary look somehow to the faces of boarders, a faint mortuary smell to even the youngest and most attractive girls. A double image, anatomical and antique. In the one the girl runs about and laughs, and in the other she lies on a bed covered by a lace shroud. It's her own skin has embroidered it.

Marion, the most attractive of them, a girl with character, has a mean look now when she sees the girl who turned her down. She flirts with a lot of the others, but she still hasn't hooked her protector. She's aware of her beauty and has no scruples. She must be twelve, maybe more. She's a pleasurable thing to look at. We are not. We already have our little adolescents' problems. She doesn't. She's enamelled, Marion. We find her eyes in cemeteries by gravestones: there's a stalk and on the stalk a violet iris. Frau Hofstetter has noticed too. Marion hasn't made her choice yet, I got the impression she was talking to Frédérique. Frédérique is not well loved; but she is respected. She hardly ever talks at table, and after lessons, if she's not on her own, she's with me. It's ridiculous for me to be sleeping in the house with the younger girls. It's the house for those who aren't considered adult, even if they only miss it by a few months. We are young up to fifteen. Frédérique sleeps on her own, with her cupboard in order, her underwear folded like altar cloths, her thoughts folded too, in their nightly starch. I say goodnight to her, she doesn't come to my room, our room, mine and the German's. Not even if the German girl's not there. But the German girl is always there, stretched out on the bed, saving herself up for her future life, not straining her adolescence. If they're happy about it in Brasil, so be it.

I'm taking piano lessons. Sometimes I think I'm playing with four hands, the other two being the hands that write the letters from Brasil. Towards the end of the first term we had the Christmas concert. December 17th. Frédérique played the piano. Beethoven, Sonata Op. 49, no. 2. They applauded her. There was a deathly silence in the room, for quite a few moments. The headmistress, the teachers, the little black girl were in the front row. Frédérique came in like an automaton, she played with a certain passion, she curtseyed like an automaton, the applause didn't seem to reach her ears. Was she a great pianist that day before Christmas, Frédérique? I think so. The way she looked impressed everyone. She showed no emotion, no vanity, no modesty, as if walking behind her own coffin. She tensed her wrists and her hands played. She was impassive, though something fugitive fluttered in the eyes and mouth. For one rare moment a violence of spirit transfigured her nevertheless immobile features. Frédérique went back to her place. I thought she had even more quality than I had imagined. There is something absolute and impregnable in certain people, it's like a distance from the world, from the living, but it's also somehow the sign of someone confronting a power we know nothing of. I felt disturbed. I'd heard Clara Haskil once. I was in the front row, I didn't want to lose anything of Clara's old age. Frédérique never asked me how she had played. I tried a few compliments, I was still moved. '*Ce n'est rien,*' she said, and we spoke no more about it. As I write now, I turn on the radio and they're playing a Beethoven concerto. I wonder if Frédérique isn't haunting me as I write about her. I turn off the radio. The silence flows back. The applause is over. Frédérique makes a slight curtsey, bows her head, and goes back to sit in her place, in the front row, next to the teachers, the little black girl. For a moment it occurs to me the little black girl is Frédérique's ancestor.

In the evening, in bed, I could still hear the applause for Frédérique. My room-mate was filing her nails. These moments seem so long, the nightly waiting as, before falling asleep, you have to invite a dream to come. Having filed and polished her nails my room-mate said: '*Gute Nacht.*' She puts her hands outside the sheets so they'll be visible when the boys come to invite her to dance. She surrenders herself to her nightly encounters with a smile, with her dimples. She came from

Nuremburg, where her father was in some GmbH. She was born just in time to see the Germans march their goosestep and the geraniums in the windows. We never talked about the war, nor about the destruction and resurrection of her city. So she had grown up in the rubble, this little nocturnal dancer. She too had a house with geraniums whose leaves curled as the Wehrmacht passed. The warriors marched beneath her window; her mother held her in her arms, a little bundle with a cap and ribbons.

Did her mother throw down flowers as though onto the stage at the theatre? They're questions I should have asked then, when we slept in the same room and only a few years had passed since the end of the war. The German girl never pronounced the word *Krieg*. Nor nazism, nor Hitler. 'Did you know Hitler?' I could have asked her. The girl's presence was an optical fact, I knew her body the way you know an illustration in a book, the way I knew my almost empty locker, I knew there was a pencil and exercise book at the bottom. A letter, a scrap of a souvenir, a handkerchief, a key. The locker, dear little mortuary of our thoughts. With its number. The little things that we thought important, that we could decide to lock up or not to lock up. Everything is optional. The authorities allowed us to use a key. It was a symbol. A symbol was part of the expensive fees. But there was no point in insisting on symbols, they're gratuitous. I never used my key. Not because I disdained the symbol: just as I had no past, so I had no secrets. Frédérique sees my locker is empty, open. I possess nothing.

Many of the girls possess diaries. With little brass studs. With keys. They think they possess their lives. My roommate has a fine voice, she sings in tune. Even during the war she must have had a good voice, together with lots of other little girls, all in tune. I think of her now and of those diaries locked up as of the dead, barely distinguishing between a human being and the paper and writing. I feel, as one does with the dead, that I've left something unfinished, a conversation, and we go on with that conversation, addressing ourselves to the dead, even if a certain haziness of memory clouds our wake over these conversations we never had. If their faces are forgotten, if certain features have faded, as in a painting, all that remains are our own voices, which we feel can't be answered. Yet, from somewhere, the dead do answer. Or they refuse to out of spite. Like stubborn schoolgirls who won't speak. We go on speaking. We are aware of moving our lips, though there is no one there. But is there any way of thinking without words? As if humanity were a language primer and every human being made up of letters. I wouldn't want to dwell very long on these reflections, which in some sense follow on from my discussions with Frédérique. Though partly they're things I'd never thought of before. I was in a wild hurry to be living in the world, and the halos of death had to do only with the past. The future meant the gates that must open and the walls that must turn into carpets. Frédérique spoke to herself. I saw her moving her lips and staring at something like emptiness. But how can emptiness be represented? Is it perhaps a falsification of everything as it was in the beginning?

Obedience and discipline set the tempo at the Bausler Institut. Day after day Frédérique gave her good example. Distracted, one might forget to greet the headmistress on meeting her in the corridor. Even in an authoritarian regime one is perhaps allowed to be lost in thought. Frédérique, who seemed to be constantly lost in thought, never forgot to greet the headmistress, or to bow her head. She even bowed her head when she saw Herr Hofstetter, husband of the headmistress, who kept himself out of the way and did the accounts.

Did Frédérique have a double life? Her conversations with me were not only profound – and I must admit here that sometimes they sapped my energy – but some of her ideas, perhaps because of the complete freedom with which she expressed them, were not strictly and safely orthodox. I was ignorant, as I have said. Frédérique gave me the impression, and I know this word makes people smile, of being a nihilist. This made her all the more intriguing to me. A nihilist with no passion, with her gratuitous laugh, a gallows laugh. I had already heard the word at home, one holiday, spoken with scorn. When Frédérique drew me into that kind of conversation, which in any event I admired, there was an atmosphere of punishment, an absence of lightness, she was not frivolous. Her face was as though honed, the flesh covering the bones became sharp. I thought of her as of a sickle moon in an oriental sky. While the people sleep she cuts off their heads. She was eloquent. She didn't talk about justice. Nor about good and evil, concepts I had heard from teachers and fellow boarders ever since I set foot in my first school at eight years old.

It was as though she talked about nothing. Her words flew. What was left after them had no wings. She never said the word God and I can barely write it down myself when I think of the silence she surrounded it with. A word spoken every day in other schools ever since I was eight. Though perhaps it isn't a word. What is the difference between a name and a word? Frédérique exhausted me. Even out in the fields, the woods, even when I pretended to be looking at the creases on the leaves, when I twisted their still damp surfaces, or got worried about the ants. She would roll the papers for her aromatic cigarettes. I postponed any serious thinking until I was out in the world, I played for time. Frédérique thought me distracted. I was in my seventh year of imprisonment. Not like her, it was her first. A novice. And maybe she had already had a couple of relationships, or crushes, given that she'd never been in boarding school, and the choice outside is wider, a market.

Frédérique was violent. I was only violent – I can think of no other way to put it – carnally. Even though I was already grown up, I wouldn't have minded a physical fight. I could have wrung my German room-mate's neck. Her languid neck offered itself, but I had been brought up a lady. Just for fun, grab hold of her to test the strength of my hands. '*Tu es une enfant.*' Was I *une enfant* because I wanted to kill just for fun? Ideas are strength, she said. I answered that I knew that too, who would doubt it? But physical exercise was important as well. It's training, I said.

After some back and forth I said she was right. I turned away, the smell of her cigarettes was too strong. What kind of tobacco did she have in her initialled silver box, for heaven's sake? It comes from Spain. From the South. And, since I would picture whatever she spoke about, I saw the Spanish coast and the sea rolling up to the grass; a small black man with a turban climbed out of a boat, the kind of figure you see on columns in antique shop windows, alive behind the glass, and offered her a packet. She had bare feet. A loose dress covered her body, on those southern shores where I had never been. But then I didn't suppose she had either.

'He who possesses a thing is he who actually has power over it.' She looked at me in amazement, she seemed impressed, she asked for an explanation. I told her it was the Swiss Civil Code. Only the law.

Then we would go back to the Bausler, and our conversations were walled up. She resumed her guise of perfect student, the authorities could trust her, a nation would have trusted her, even if nations don't trust, but follow. Frédérique's life was not important to her.

As a student Frédérique did not win the affection of her peers. I don't recall seeing anyone going up to her and speaking to her for more than five minutes. Her pigeon hole had no notes in it. She was avoided out of respect. If I had seen her with someone, I would have had the chance to get an idea of the kind of person she might eventually be interested in, and, since I kept constant watch over her, I was able to conclude, with a certain gloating joy, that she was more interested in ideas than in human beings. Though one can hardly speak of human beings in a boarding school. At table sometimes I would hear her laugh her gratuitous laugh that haunted me in my sleep. I turned, and everybody's face was serious.

It seems pointless repeating that I took no interest in any of the other girls; having said which, I could, if questioned, perhaps admit that I was in love with Frédérique. We never spoke of love, the way most people do. But we were certain that it was predestined. We never spoke about personal things, about our families, about money, about dreams. I knew her father was a banker in Geneva. A Protestant family. (Mine likewise. Not the one in Brasil.) Nothing about her mother. They never came to see her. It seemed Frédérique had a secret. I didn't enquire. By now, nearing the end of the first term, we were united, I didn't have to go and look for her or to knock on her door and say: '*Je te dérange?*'

Fresh letters arrived from Brasil, fresh orders: it was hoped that Miss X would finally find some friends. She had been growing up too lonely and wild. So much I was told by the headmistress, Frau Hofstetter, as though she were the manager of some dating agency for lonely hearts. To which she had replied that: Miss X (myself) had made friends with the best student in the school, a girl of great talent and a pianist. Perhaps she would become a Brontë and the Bausler Institut would be proud to have had her as a student. Miss X could not have chosen better. Everybody admired the girl and she accepted praise with modesty and simplicity. This friendship could not be anything but positive. Miss X still studies very little, she takes no interest in her work, but she has made some progress in French literature. The head mistress omitted to mention that the student in question spoke French and not German, as had been ordered from Brasil. But omission is not deceit.

Frédérique knew about my morning walks. Every day I got up at five; my room-mate was asleep. The school was cloaked in a subterranean wind, life was rotting, or regenerating itself. Making no noise, I passed close to her bed to go to the bathroom, a small space with two big washbasins, one for the German, the other for me. How many times we must have washed together. Frédérique hadn't been able to bring herself to wash next to a room-mate. They took turns. But now Frédérique sleeps on her own. Since she is so deserving in everything, they have given her a room to herself. It wasn't a problem for me, I didn't find washing together too intimate, or worthy of note, or unpleasant. It was difficult to find it so when you always dressed and undressed in front of your room-mate, and had done so for term after term, year after year. We washed our feet in the washbasins too, but Frédérique hadn't even been able to wash her feet with her room-mate. We washed very fast, a bit like soldiers, or life prisoners. The showers were in common and you had to queue.

In any event, it would have been difficult to have taken turns with the German girl. She was always washing or she would stand for hours to look at herself in the mirror above the basins. And she spoke to the mirrors. Because of course they answer. What's more, I was more chatty with my German room-mate when we were washing, I almost liked her then, with her perfumed skin, her slightly thick calves. They must have overdeveloped her legs making her walk in the mountains, I've seen little girls dragged along furiously, right to the peak. Her ankles were slim, but still had something rough and robust about them, like a *Bursch*, I told her in German, a working boy. At night she gave me the impression she was dressing for a dance, but I could also imagine her going off hunting in her lederhosen.

Frédérique listened to my descriptions, since I couldn't help talking about bodies, with a serious, questioning expression. You see monsters everywhere, she said. I saw shapes that I couldn't forget. When I told her about the headmistress's body – her thin legs that grew thicker at the groin, the broad muscliness of her bust, she started to laugh. Did she laugh, Frédérique? Her theory was that I must find others repulsive. She said I was an ascetic when it came to female bodies. I told her how years ago, in boarding school of course, a girl had climbed into my bed. Her breasts were just forming, they were still muscly. She felt hot, I threw her out, she fell like a sack.

'*Tu es une enfant*,' said Frédérique again. I knew almost nothing of the war, I knew that the cellars in our villa had been filled with food supplies in case of a German invasion. They also served as a shelter for seventy people. There were still some supplies left in the fifties. None of my family, who took turns at having me for the holidays, ever had the time or inclination to tell me the history of the world and its iniquities. I didn't ask. I was often distracted. Distracted by nothing. With Frédérique I was constantly having to concentrate on precise things.

Many girls had had crushes or flirtations or had been to dances. I had only danced in hotels, in Mont-Cervin di Zermatt, in Rigi Kaltbad, in Celerina and Wengen, with older men who asked me out of politeness toward my father, who didn't dance. More often than dancing I would take part in games, wearing my evening dress sent from Brasil and my black varnished shoes. Gloomy games. I held a sort of rod with a ring attached that you had to lower into a bottle. My father and I were so much alone, sometimes in the evenings we went out to amuse ourselves in the *Stube*. And here again I was waiting to get out into the world. Sadly, almost without impatience. Time was out of joint.

I couldn't tell Frédérique about this. Even if she hadn't lived quite so much as she seemed to have, all the same her tone of voice and a sort of intensity about her made you believe she had. She could have written a love story from a cold heart, like an old woman reminiscing. Or a blind woman. Sometimes her pupils would fix on one spot and stare and I didn't dare interrupt. '*Tu rêves.*' She wasn't dreaming. She was rolling herself a cigarette and closing it with her tongue.

I often spent my free time in her room, almost always standing up. She didn't lie on her bed like my roommate, she didn't take her pullover off like the German girl who got hot. She was tidy, Frédérique, obsessively tidy, like her exercise books, like her handwriting, like her cupboards. I was convinced that it was a strategy for not attracting attention, for hiding, for not mixing with the others, or simply keeping her distance. '*Tu es possédée par l'ordre.*' '*J'aime l'ordre,*' she answered, smiling. I understood those children who jump from the top floor of a school simply to do something disordered, and I told her. Order was like ideas, something you possessed, something that possessed you. I would have liked to have met her father, but he died.

Apples and pears on the branches of the Appenzell, pastureland and barbed wire. A boy with a St Gallen lace veil hanging round his shoulders. On a house the motto: 'Accept in peace what fortune brings.' Early in the morning I walked on the hills. From up there I could observe my mental dominions. It was my appointment with Nature. I climbed even higher, and below, on the horizon, I could see Lake Constance. Where later I was to go as a boarder in another college, on a small island, which we would walk right round every day in a column two by two. Perhaps it will seem obsessive, that walk round the island every day between one and three; even monks walk around their cloisters, eyes circling as they move. I ask myself what might not become obsessive. It was an idyll, an obsessive idyll. In the school on the island, a religious institution, a girl read out loud during meals. When she finished, Mater gave us permission to talk. We returned to pagan life.

All of a sudden the voices, the rhythm of knives and forks. The Germans talking, laughing, eating, helping themselves to seconds, of *Blutwurst* too. I had seconds of the dessert, the rhubarb. There was no blood there. The most commonly used word was *freilich*. Can I do this, can I have permission? '*Ja, freilich. Freilich.*' (It meant 'Of course,' but it also meant: 'freely').

Mater Hermenegild, she was called. She was cheerful, she played with us. In the courtyard Mater raised her arms with strength and joy to catch a ball and she was a good runner. We could do what we wanted, on the island. Except go out on our own. Always stay together. If possible in a column, two by two. In even numbers. The girls immediately smelt out anyone anti-social. When it rained we would all be kept in the same room. We listened to the radio. Some girls read. A *Krimi Roman*. Others stared, lost, misty. The older girls, Germans, cooked. Bavarian lace makers. Mater Hermenegild kept guard. She kept guard over liberty. Those who weren't enjoying themselves idled away the hours. The bathrooms looked out on a narrow, dark alleyway and a wall. The water had already been run for us. Very hot. I felt as if I were getting into it with my clothes on. There were two churches, Catholic and Protestant. We had freedom of religion on Lake Constance. Just for a change I went to the Protestant one. Even though the order from Brazil was: Catholic. She orders, I obey, she steers me through the terms, it's all written in letters and stamps, bells with no sound. Dispatches.

Frédérique was likewise asleep while I took my walks. The crows flew low over the steep grassy slopes, hideous, boastful, cruel. I had compared them to our adolescence as they searched for a place in the earth round the school to sink their claws into. In half an hour I was already high above, filling my lungs with the cold air. The universe seemed mute. I didn't want Frédérique, nor thought about her. She read at night, perhaps she had only just fallen asleep. In the morning she was a bit stiff, shadows under her eyes. Up on the hill I was in a state you might describe as 'ill-happiness'. A state that required solitude, a state of exhilaration and quiet selfishness, a cheerful vendetta. I had the impression that this exhilaration was an initiation, that the sickness in the happiness was due to a magical novitiate, a rite. Then it went wrong. I didn't feel anything particular any more. Every landscape constructed its own niche and shut itself away there.

I hurried back down, I was back in my room again, the German girl still hadn't opened the window, her dreams, however light and pretty, staled the air, and perhaps the dashing young men who invited her to dance, taking her votive hands in theirs, were breathing it too. She had barely finished dressing herself with those hands, her blouse was still unbuttoned, she didn't want to go to class, said the sleepy, sincere expression on her face.

She was one of those girls who should have had a different life. She was conscientious, full of good will, the same good will her parents had had, though they were more hard-working. Her smile, fragile, idiotic and affectionate, suggested vulnerability in the face of scholastic duties. She liked to feel herself coddled by the cosy air of the bedroom, she was sensual in a docile way, it was an effort for her to learn a couple of verses off by heart, and sometimes even to understand them. She had established once and for all that the girl she shared her room with was interested in the German expressionists, who as a result were becoming a disaster: to please that girl she gave her books and postcards. She was one of those people who never forget a concept once they have grasped it. When she got something into her head, a little late perhaps, she couldn't help but repeat it.

There was also a protracted childishness about her, not the monstrous, poetic kind of childishness, but something sham and lazy. She was slow getting up; when I got back from my morning forays her bed was still warm.

The girl she had chosen as a friend was the same: a Bavarian girl, daughter of a managing director, an only child. They would meet after lessons, around five o'clock. At six my German room-mate was already back in our room. Sometimes her eyes wandered across the ceiling. She got a letter which said that a cousin of hers was dying. It took him a few weeks to die and she got a lot of letters. During those weeks the German girl seemed to wake up from her torpor. She imagined his death throes, and in the meantime she tied the letters in a pink ribbon; she tied the knot again, she had pulled it too tight; she threw the envelopes away, then got them back again, smoothed them out, added them to the letters, pulled the ribbon tight, tied the knot again with a bow. She didn't keep them in the baroque German box, but on her bedside table where she kept the photographs of her parents and a few sweets. In the drawer was a Bible, school property. Finally an envelope with black edging arrived. It wasn't handed out at mealtimes, as was usually the case. Instead the headmistress gave it to her personally. She sat at her table, looked at it, opened it, read it, put it back in its envelope and turned to look at me. Her gestures had a rhythm to them, it was as though someone had suspended time. She opened the pack, undid the pink ribbon, slipped in the black-edged envelope with the others and tied knot and bow again with angelic pedantry.

It was snowing in Teufen, snowing in the Appenzell. Life at the Bausler Institut was quiet. Outside, the sound of shovels. The little black girl coughed, the young boarder, daughter of an African head of state received with all honours by the Bausler Institut. The other pupils felt those honours were excessive. We were all lined up as if we each of us had a sentry box beside us, standing to attention to receive the President, the wife of the President and the little girl. Frau Hofstetter was as excited as a farmyard animal. We wondered if perhaps this was out of submissiveness to an African state, or if such a welcome would be extended to presidents in general. It is almost admirable that in the Swiss Confederation the name of the President passes unobserved and likewise his charming person. There had been a President of the Confederation in our family, but he would have refused such honours. His gravestone is very modest. Lenin, who had been a guest, was known as a hothead in the Confederation. There were no hotheads in the boarding school at Teufen. There was peace in the Appenzell and likewise in the houses of the families of the boarders, in the furnishings and in the mirrors. The girls were fortunate, if one can consider this good fortune. Some spiteful older people curse instead of answering the greetings of the girls on their walks. '*Grüss Gott,*' the German girls said. But they don't want God, those old people. They don't want good wishes, they suspect they are being insulted.

The girls went down into the village, rounding the bend in the path where like a curse the word *Töchterinstitut* was written on a low wall. And the nordic light, harmful and crazed, dwells on the wall. In a window the lace curtains twitch, eyes find themselves trapped there, as if it were the horizon. The headmistress respected each of us and our families. She keeps guard. Someone is suffering from *Weltschmerz*. And is mocked.

From then on the little black girl coughed. She had learnt to speak German. Frau Hofstetter, the headmistress, read *Max und Moritz* to her: that's how you amuse children in the Appenzell. Frau Hofstetter takes care of the girl; to protect her throat she does up the top button of her blue coat with its dark velvet collar and cuffs. The little girl has grown sad. Frau Hofstetter doesn't know what to do to distract her. Perhaps she should have warned the President. 'Dear and Honoured President, Your Daughter is bored with everything.' The boredom of children is pure desperation. Generally, they say, children amuse themselves with next to nothing, and one wonders what that next to nothing might be. Or they amuse themselves with nothing at all. And what was that nothing at all that no longer amused the little black girl? 'The hanged men go ding dong,' says the refrain of an old American song. The little girl didn't sing, or talk to herself. Sometimes she skipped in the yard, lifting a thin knee, or she ran around in a circle. We all have to bear and atone for the games that were not our own. A bit of a sleepwalker, she let her spirit rove. Shortly before Christmas, amidst the candles, they asked her to sing *Stille Nacht*. Frau Hofstetter pushed her into the middle of the room. The French teacher was sitting at the piano with her squat, masculine hands. The little girl turned her old woman's eyes to our tables; she looked like the last of her race, the candlelight streaked her pupils. She sang in a thin voice, a voice that came from a body that wasn't her own, disinterred. Frau Hofstetter clapped vigorously and kissed her forehead. *Mein Kind, mein Kind*, she whispered and caressed her hair, her thin pigtails, her shoulders, her narrow little body and flared skirt. She counted the fingers of her hand as if she were a doll. The girl let herself be caressed like a corpse.

'The black girl's really talented,' my room-mate says, 'she's so musical.' She has never heard people sing like that in Germany. She's generous with her compliments, my room-mate. How gracefully she could exaggerate. Was she really sure the girl had sung so well? She sounded out of tune to us. 'Out of tune?' she said. And she repeated the phrase, brooding. Stubbornly she shook her head; no, she wasn't out of tune. But . . . But in the middle of the refrain she had coughed. 'What do you think,' she asked. 'Might she be ill?' 'She could have TB.' 'What? You think she could be ill?' As she spoke, her enthusiasm for the black girl's musical talent waned.

My room-mate is worried now. Chest problems are infectious. In Germany they've got rid of TB. She had heard someone say so. I asked her if someone in her family, one of her grandparents, had died of TB. *Nein, nein*, everybody in her family had died of old age. *Niemand war krank*. No one ill. She had forgotten the envelope with the black edging, but she must have felt that that death wasn't part of the rule. The rule was that members of her family left the world because they had reached the natural conclusion of their lives. Her father and mother would grow old, very old, and then the inevitable. My room-mate was healthy enough herself, she ate lots of cakes, she gobbled up everything at table, she never had a cold. She got between the sheets and assumed her nightly pose and it was only natural that her *Gute Nacht* would be followed by the morning's *Guten Tag*: a regular succession of segments which fit together. But now the black girl's illness had sneaked into her head, while her musical talent had slipped out.

She said that blacks have musical talent and can tap dance very well; she had learnt to tap dance too and she liked it. She did a few steps, heavy, but technically right.

They could dance a duet. Maybe for the show at the end of the school year. Boarding schools always celebrate the end of the school year. In her head she set about organising the show, in the school yard. She assigned parts, she even gave me a part, I was to be a gipsy, *Du bist eine Zigeunerin,* her face was glowing. And with an inspired expression she said she could do Klopstock too; do a tap dance and something from Klopstock, her, the German girl, and her parents would come, everybody's parents had to come. She assigned places to the audience. Frédérique, your friend, she said, could play for the *finale.* A little gavotte, or the funeral march. I listened. Yes of course I listened to the German girl. Every people has its talent, every people has its bloody karma, every boarder has her tap dance, and she had hers too; she wouldn't let up with her ferocious glee, her determination and greedy gaiety. Soon she would be crying. Chary tears in her eyes. Her legs bent. She sat down, overcome by her own mirth.

Frau Hofstetter's husband, a weak character, wouldn't have dared to caress the girl. His wife, who was the headmistress and a strong character, could take a fancy to one boarder, detest another. In his laziness Herr Hofstetter thought they were all equal, all charming; after a year they showed faint signs of getting older. He came a poor second to his wife's little crushes, his wife's chaste crushes. They were both chaste, if by chaste we mean a worthy indifference to sex, or a lack of appetite. Frau Hofstetter had a propensity or two, as she had shown her husband during the first months of their marriage, thirty years ago. His wife hadn't been so big then, she'd been slim almost, much taller than him, with a ladylike gutsiness that won her respect. Her chin was prominent, her jaws wide, her eyes small and a little evil. She was always tidy and well meaning. Her bearing gave off that unmistakable aura of the teacher by profession and vocation, the iron-handed lay teacher.

They didn't have a long engagement. She had decided to marry him and in bed she was brisk. Her husband divided mankind into two: the weak and the strong. A boarding school is a strong institution, since in a sense it is founded on blackmail. Likewise his marriage. He needed that big woman whose bosom filled out when she breathed and who showed her husband the same indulgent severity she showed to the girls. His office was a small corner room, the bursar's office. Business was good. But sometimes he felt ill at ease in that entirely female world. He would find himself talking to the tennis, gymnastics and geography master, a dry man with precocious wrinkles and a tight mouth, as though biting into the last mouthful of youth left to him. Withered before his time.

Sometimes the two men went into the village together, the master walking with a sporty elastic step, the fake youthfulness he was cultivating, chest pushed out in a fine curve. Even his thighs gave the impression of a handsome young man from a distance, a pretty rare sight in that village inhabited by the old. From close up you could make out his skull. The two went to the café together, but they had nothing to say to each other. Maybe they felt they were damned or forgotten, or maybe they liked being there, rejects from the rest of the world. All you need is a fleeting thought flying up in the air that becomes your own; but if you don't grasp it you feel even more alone than before. Those girls had their whole lives in front of them, and Frau Hofstetter's husband knew they dreamed of having a good time. He had nothing in front of him now. Every year there were new girls who dreamed of all the fantastic things that life would give them, that his wife promised them. The future was theirs. He sensed this like a thorn in his side. Sometimes he had thought of taking revenge on their dreams. He knew how to go about it. On the other hand, he had grown fond of the little black girl. He felt there was some affinity between them. He was stirred in his bursar's office when he saw her alone in the yard or the garden, raising her knees and skipping joylessly. The girl stops and looks imperiously at the ground, digging.

A new arrival always arouses a certain amount of curiosity. The girl came towards the end of January. We spoke to each other by chance. Actually we didn't speak at all: we burst out laughing. She was a bit like Gilda. Her red hair was magnificent, a prey, it looked photographed. When she came into the *Speisesaal* there was a sudden silence. Knives and forks remained suspended in the air. Sailors would have whistled. Frédérique waited for me for our afternoon walk. I arrived late. *Tu as vu la nouvelle?* I had, I had indeed.

Immediately we changed the subject. Maybe to Baudelaire. He had had a creole woman. The redhead looked a bit creole too. That evening over dinner we joked as if we were old friends. The other girls round us stopped talking and followed our chatter, all eyes and ears. There was a Spanish girl next to me who ate mostly yoghurt for her waistline. 'Come up to my room,' said Micheline, that was what the new girl was called. She embraced me, she gave me a kiss, the way she might have kissed her horse. I went to her room and she told me most of her life story, as if it were a *carnet de bal.*

I explained that I'd have to go because I slept in the other house. Which house? For the younger girls. She burst out laughing. You, one of the younger girls! But that's outrageous. She said it as though on stage in front of an audience. I hurried out and went past Frédérique's room, I didn't dare go in. It was too late. At quarter past nine everybody had to be in their own room. I went to sleep in an excellent mood. My room-mate, who had finished brushing out her hair said: '*Sehr elegant, rassig, die Neue.*' Elegant wasn't the right word perhaps. Though a beauty like that doesn't need to be elegant. It was Frédérique was elegant.

Micheline was infatuated by her beauty, she carried it round with her like a tropical bird. Frédérique was more beautiful than Micheline, but she never exulted over it. Micheline, who was less refined, couldn't help but offer her beauty, simply and spontaneously, to everybody, exulting. She was an extrovert, that was the first trait that attracted me. And her cheerfulness. She immediately showed me all her clothes. It was as if the sun shone out of her cupboards. When she embraced me, and I let her, I felt her strong healthy body against mine, like a wet nurse. Everything was soft and young and athletic. She embraced me the way she would have embraced a crowd. Without sin or vice. A real companionly embrace I might almost say, even though the term has lost its old sense. She was a comrade. Not like Frédérique and me, who didn't dare so much as to touch each other, or kiss each other. Horror. Perhaps because troubled by our desire, troubled because it didn't fit in with the images we had formed of each other.

On a number of occasions I did feel the impulse to caress her, but her stiffness turned me away. Micheline's little eyes had an amazed, vacuous, calm expression. When she got angry they became even smaller, as if the irises had dried up. It was the whole impression that made her beautiful. I got into the habit of seeing her in my free time. Most of what we said to each other was nonsense; there wasn't much it was worth talking seriously about. But you could laugh about anything. She didn't study, she didn't care about anything. She was going to give a huge ball with her daddy. She didn't care about her mother, perhaps she was dead. You forget the dead. There was just Daddy. She would invite me to her ball. I would be her best friend. Hadn't we already been best friends for a while? *Depuis toujours*. We would write to each other.

She invited me to stay in her villa as long as I wanted, Daddy would like me. And Daddy would flirt with me. He flirted with all her schoolfriends. Did my daddy flirt with my friends? My daddy has never met a friend of mine. Was I jealous perhaps, did I stop him seeing them?

What was my daddy's villa like? My daddy lived in a hotel. So I didn't have a house. Yes, I did, but not with Daddy. Her daddy was young and when they went out together she made herself up so she would look like his girlfriend. I thought of my daddy, of the innumerable hotels of our holidays, winter and summer, and that old man with his white hair and ice-clear, sad eyes. Which would gradually become my eyes.

And Micheline talked, she made plans for the future, always the same plans. What mattered was that there should be movement, confusion, applause and Daddy. I neglected Frédérique, I hardly ever went to our meetings. When Micheline put her hand on my shoulders in front of everybody and Frédérique saw, I felt ashamed. I felt ill at ease. I was at ease when I was in Micheline's room, or alone with her, but I didn't want Frédérique to see me. And Frédérique saw me, I sensed her sad gaze directed at me, a reproach almost. I had fun with Micheline, even if her cheerfulness and her daddy were boring me, but you can enjoy a fatuous cheerfulness despite the boredom, a funereal fervour.

What Micheline wanted from life was to have a good time, and wasn't that what I wanted too? Sometimes it upset me deeply that I was neglecting Frédérique, and other times it gave me a kind of satisfaction. I was doing it on purpose. And I saw Frédérique, exactly as she had been, never talking to anyone, detached from the rest of us, detached from the world, and I wanted to go and talk to her, to tell her that it was a joke for me, a distraction, that she should let me play. As soon as I had these thoughts, I did the opposite. Was I perhaps punishing Frédérique for my love?

Three months had gone, the second term was almost over and I had deserted Frédérique. Every evening, when I lay in bed and the German girl slept with her curls neatly spread on her pillow, I passed the time with Frédérique; we would be walking together and sometimes, without realising, I would speak out loud. I'd decide to go and see her next morning. All would be as it had been before. The next morning I changed my mind. If I met her in the corridor, she smiled without stopping. She didn't even give me the chance to say anything. She slipped away from me like a shadow; if we were in the same room, I was unable to joke with Micheline and I would stare and stare at Frédérique, hoping for a sign or a nod. She was impassive.

Frédérique never sought me out during those months. On the contrary it was me with my old woman's hands who sought to cling to her. One day we heard that her father had died. And Frédérique would be going. That day I learnt what terror was. Something irrevocable. I ran to her room. She spoke to me very sweetly, she was going to her father's funeral and she wouldn't be coming back to the Bausler Institut. I went with her to the small station in Teufen. It was hot, the sky was blue, a distant haze veiled the infinite. The landscape, enchanting. It was three in the afternoon. She hardly spoke at all, walking fast. I was afraid and I walked behind her, catching up with her in little bursts.

I declared myself, I declared my love. More than to her I spoke to the landscape. The train looked like a toy, it left. '*Ne sois pas triste.*' She left me a note. I had lost what was most important in my life, the sky was still blue, oblivious, everything yearned for peace and happiness, the landscape was idyllic, like idyllic, desperate adolescence. The landscape seemed to protect us, the small white houses of Appenzell, the fountain, the sign *Töchterinstitut*, it was as if the place hadn't been affected by human distortions. Can one feel disorientated in an idyll? An atmosphere of catastrophe covered the landscape. The irremediable came home to me in one of the most beautiful, transparent days of the year. I had lost Frédérique. I asked her to promise to write. She said yes, but I sensed that she wouldn't. I immediately wrote her an impassioned letter, not knowing what I was writing. I waited for a letter from her. I sensed that she would never write to me. It wouldn't be like her. She was the kind that disappear.

And that was what Frédérique did, she disappeared.

I went back to the school and spent my time with my misery, which is a way like any other of spending time. I read the note she had given me at the station, two small sheets of chequered paper seven centimetres square. Her handwriting slept as if on a stone in this paper wall. Practising patiently, I had learnt to copy her handwriting, I had perfected perfection itself, with the discipline of falsehood. I read her note as though it were an ornament. Waves. She spoke to me of metaphysics, she didn't mention our friendship. That exhortation, that deception, that anonymous tone, ecumenical and cloistered, would have done as well for anyone. In the last line she 'embraced me with affection': a formal expression, a static gesture. We never embraced, nor did we use the word affection when we spoke to each other. Her note was a sermon in a way, she recognised certain qualities I had together with an inclination to destruction. I didn't keep the two sheets of paper like a relic, nor did I tear them up in that dark, restless spring, tossing them away into the void. For a while I kept them in my pocket, then they got crumpled, the paper shrivelled up, it tore, the ink faded. Frédérique's words were headed for burial. We can put a cross against certain words and place them in our minds with a file card.

I went home for the Easter holidays, to a hotel. Some people invited us for lunch, they showed us slides of a trip with ruins and landscapes and themselves. They were an old couple of exemplary virtue, well-meaning, rich, discreetly tight, discreetly polite, opposed, especially the wife, to good humour and good living, if such a thing as good living exists. Dry and stiff, in long shapeless clothes, her hair pulled straight back, the wife did not look kindly upon my youth from her shrunken head and colourless eyes. Out of bonhommie or indulgence the husband would let a deep laugh gurgle up from his well-defined, slightly fleshy mouth, if there was anything to laugh about, and his eyes became sly, almost as though laughter were connected with malice. On his waistcoat he wore the pocket watch of his grandfather, or some dead relative. He looked at it frequently, weighing up the time in his hand. His dark suit had given long service and conferred a certain dignity.

In the garden, which looked down on the lake, an Alsatian behind a fence paced furiously up and down, snarling. The following day, a white foggy day, father and daughter were taken for a trip round the lake. The woman, supervising the maid, prepared a picnic. Everything was calculated to guarantee a happy outing. The mute expression on the lady's face, brimming with a sense of duty as she peered at the meagre rays of sun as if at a trap, said as much. Two hours later the trip was over. They were my father's best friends.

From the moment we entered the Bausler Institut all we thought about was the moment we would leave it. And now that moment had arrived. Sooner than expected, mentally, but on schedule according to the calendar. The fervour of the spring announced the end, the meadows were covered with flowers. It began to get hot, the *Föhn*. The first mowing striped the grass. The windows were always open and the air was heavy with a sense of bitterness and fate. The year took its leave. And, despite all this, nothing happened. The German girl is hot, she sits near the window.

Micheline promised everybody invitations and balls in her villa. She changed dresses every day, her blouses made us look at our own, which were simpler and more suitable for school, with dismay. But it was Daddy who chose Micheline's dresses. Daddy whom we were soon to meet, but we were already having fun with Daddy, all our jokes were about Daddy, and Micheline never stopped talking about her Daddy, her father seeped out of her flesh like a second voice. And your mother? they asked her. Oh, Maman isn't around. Is she dead though? Not exactly, Micheline said. And if she realised that some girl or other was worried she would take her by the arm. No one's died, dear. But there was bitterness in her eyes now.

Sometimes I would walk to the little station in Teufen and stand there to listen: I heard Frédérique's brief, philistine farewell: Adieu, a brief, sober sound. Farewells have distant ancestors and the hills and fields cover them with chaff and dust.

I hadn't been able to say anything to her about her father's death, it was as if he'd never existed. But even those who don't exist die. And that's why Frédérique left the school and me. I saw no emotion in her eyes. Nor was I moved, by the death of her father: it was Frédérique's sudden departure scared me. The banker had come between us.

Frédérique was folding her clothes, which had already been laid out with the arms crossed over each other. The cupboards were empty. I attempted a vague '*désolée*'. Frédérique shut her suitcase.

Meanwhile my father was making notes in a book

bound in blue cloth entitled '*Mein Lebenslauf*', and containing the dates relative to my life. As far as the Bausler Institut is concerned the book offers the following record: his visit 31 October, dinner at St. Gallen. 9 November, his visit. 17 December, Christmas Party in school. 3 January, I visit him. 25 April, Teufen. 8–10 May, I visit him. And these notes had been going on and on since I was eight. I received visits, I made visits. The names of the schools changed. A series of repetitions. Only here and there a name changes, a different village. But Frédérique's name is not to be found in the *Lebenslauf* with the blue cloth binding. I was still sure that the notes were premonitions, looking forward to the life I would live after school. I was almost fifteen now, and the book had filled up. Without my knowing. With a senile girlhood.

Frau Hofstetter called in her dog, a bulldog, who, like the boarders, liked to bask in the sun. When the bulldog was obedient she cleaned his slobbers, saying: '*Mein Kind.*' I heard Herr Hofstetter call his wife, the headmistress, '*Mutti.*' It seems that in the Appenzell in spring drowsy affections are reawakened, animals and little girls are pampered. The proprietor of the café and stationer's greets them with a new and heavy smile.

There's a breath of resurrection in the air, murder transformed into a state of grace. Pairs of young ladies sit at the café. Despite its being spring, hardly anyone goes by. It's hot. Teufen is all theirs. Marion has made her choice. She walks by with her friend. She said: I want that one. And the girl, a generous girl, has already given her a part of herself. They walk together as Frédérique and I walked together in months past, but Frédérique has gone. They walk together as the first boarders did no sooner than the Bausler Institut was built in Canton Appenzell.

During the distribution of the post in the large and noble dining hall, we watch the headmistress's hands as she gives out the letters, slowly, cautiously. She would pretend to make a mistake and give me my envelope last. I recognise the stamps, the dignitaries of the country, from way off. The envelopes from Brazil were light and the air mail stamps had their perforations nibbled up, like fruit by insects. I knew Frédérique wouldn't write. But I persevered in the pleasure of taking my sadness to the limit, the way one does with some practical joke. The pleasure of disappointment. It wasn't new to me. I had been relishing it ever since I was eight years old, a boarder in my first, religious, school. And perhaps they were the best years, I thought. Those years of discipline. There was a kind of elation, faint but constant throughout all those days of discipline, the sweet days of discipline.

We all wore blue berets with the initials of the boarding school. I was at the station, in my uniform and beret. I was waiting for the train from the Gothard. It would stop for three minutes beside the windy platform. They let me go on my own, they checked that I was impeccable, my shoes polished. There I stood, spruced up, to see her pass by, go through the station, then she would be taking the *Andrea Doria* and sailing across the ocean, my maman. Opposite, the second-class buffet in the station was like our own shrouded rooms, or a nursing home. I seemed to see destitute people stretched out, the disorder of a destiny that breathed on the windowpanes, seen, from the other side of the railway lines, like some sequence in a novelised life.

So there I was, with my beret and the initials, on the other side of the world, on that side where one is protected and watched over. I foresaw the pain, the desertion, with an acute sense of joy. I greeted the train, the carriages, the compartments, all split up, the burnished alcoves, the velvet, the porcelain passengers, those strangers, those obscure companions. Joy over pain is malicious, there's poison in it. It's a vendetta. It is not so angelic as pain. I stood a while on the platform of a squalid station. The wind wrinkled the dark lake and my thoughts as it swept on the clouds, chopped them up with its hatchet; between them you could just glimpse the Last Judgement, finding each of us guilty of nothing.

That school was destroyed. It doesn't exist any more. When I found out, I couldn't hide my satisfaction. I had thought it immortal. Even the majestic marble staircase and the beds surrounded by gauze drapes promising candour and death, had been demolished. I told Frédérique, for she was the one person I could tell, how the building's destruction had given me '*un parfait contentement*' (as it says on one of the tarot cards). I also said to

Frédérique that maybe it had been our thoughts, or the vibrations given off at the age of innocence, that had destroyed it. She said that innocence was a modern invention.

We joked, we wondered how long the Bausler Institut would last. And it seemed as if it must last forever, for future generations, in radiant peace. Standing in the shadow of the school wall, Frédérique jokes. The shadows of the trees, like banners, exalt this place that seems immortal.

I noticed she had a dull, leaden, glazed look about her, something unpleasant in her eyes, which would seem indigo sometimes, but in fact were moss coloured, swamp coloured.

Micheline, the cheerful, fun-loving Belgian, calls to me. She doesn't realise that cheerfulness can become dreary. Cheerfulness is difficult to handle. Micheline takes off her pullover, she's hot, she helps me to put it on, I'm cold. We lift our arms together, I feel her warmth, and her warmth is cheerful. Her skin, her perfume. Have fun, Frédérique seemed to be saying, but she would never have actually said it. Except to someone at death's door. Micheline laughed. Her little teeth were all even, exact, her forehead low and her mouth made up when she went to the village, to Teufen. The cripple was there, and two pale gentlemen with pitchforks, as if they were off to swear an oath, the baker, who smelt of custard cream and puff pastry, the ageing women with their braids and buns. The child with the tin whistle, and the windows framed in white. A belltower with a golden ball on top. The village street finished where it began. *Wir wollen kein Glück*. We want no luck, you hear people say in the village.

Daddy has promised Micheline a fortune. Daddy swept away her worries, she mustn't have disturbing thoughts. Daddy invites everyone to his big party in Belgium. I saw Frédérique from a distance, untouched by the other girls' happiness, their fun. Frédérique keeps her eyes down on a book.

At Carnival Micheline and I danced together. All the boarders have to dance. Everyone was wearing their carnival masks, it was a must to wear your carnival masks. Frau Hofstetter and her husband, the bursar, sat calm and still as they watched us, like the agents of a lenient police force. The Hofstetters man and wife sat together in the dining hall, specially done up for the ball. Streamers on the walls, fancy decorations and candyfloss. Frédérique didn't join in. She excused herself and went up to her room. Micheline moved her hips, keeping time. Perhaps cheerfulness is getting to be tiresome for her too. Her low forehead beaded with sweat, her red cheeks. Daddy will wash her face, a face about to wither. Her beauty has become a parody. The old face is already sketched out in the young, and exhaustion lurks behind cheerfulness, the way some babies are scarcely born before they're reminding you of the grandparent who just died.

Only the little black girl was sad, a sadness without respite, controlled and measured. I watched her. It was the sadness of desperation I thought. She doesn't let the headmistress hold her hand any more these days. Her hands touch nothing but the emptiness of her thoughts. I saw her gathering yellow flowers, she held them warm and drowsy in her arms. She cuddled them as if they were a little baby, singing a soft lullaby, her eyes dull and ecstatic. Then she threw them on the ground. She buried them. She was the tiny dispatch rider of a routed army.

She looked around, her body moving slowly with the stiffness and bleariness of someone shocked by a bad dream. 'Good morning,' I greeted her. But she didn't answer. We had never spoken to her, Frédérique and I. Her life at the Bausler Institut seemed to be exclusively a matter for the headmistress. She took private lessons, she never had a friend, and if we heard her voice at Christmas it was only because she was forced to sing *Stille Nacht*. As far as most of the girls were concerned she was the President's daughter, and they made her pay for that. There are times when one wants everyone to be equal and one imposes a sort of imaginary democracy. If a girl is received, as the black girl was, with flags and pomp of every variety, and if there is applause for an African head of state, then that applause will be held against her.

By tacit agreement and right from the beginning the girls in a school will choose their pariah with careless affection. Not because one passes the word to the others:

it's a general impulse. It's the evil eye, like a divining rod, seeking out its victim. With no real reason to explain the choice but bad luck. The black girl did nothing but wrap herself in it, give it an aura of truth, as though imposed by destiny. She was pining away, visibly. She began to cough, she no longer spoke, and when she leafed through a book Frau Hofstetter had given her, her alabaster fingers came to rest on an illustration: a mound of earth and a cross.

I felt friendly toward her in my last two days at school. I followed her around. Somebody so unhappy, I thought, won't notice that she's being spied on, and spy is what I did. It wasn't so much her I was watching, though, as her unhappiness. Just as at the beginning of the school year I had kept my eye on Frédérique, so now I observed the black girl. My attention was entirely concentrated on her, on that one thing: unhappiness. I thought of the graves in the wall, the graves that nest in our minds. The black girl didn't notice anything.

It was as though I were looking at someone already dead. With her carefully twisted braids, the round eyes that had lost their spell, a sickly smile, as if of constant farewell. They made her wear a blue cotton jacket. A Swiss driver came to get her. They sat her in a limousine. The powers that be were lined up: Frau Hofstetter with gleaming teardrops in her eyes, and her husband. Two girls were playing tennis and I was walking along the road towards the village. At a bend the car passed. Like a robot, the black girl nodded and her hand sketched a goodbye.

Micheline went too. She kissed and hugged everyone, a great, emphatic goodbye to the school, to the time she was leaving behind, to her laughter, which perhaps would generate other laughter. Her hair fluttered in the wind. She ran to me to kiss me too, folding her arms round me like wings. And I mustn't forget her great ball, the most fantastic extravagant party in Europe, and her daddy. Her daddy would flirt with all of us, in Belgium. '*C'est promis.*' '*C'est promis,*' I answered. And it was goodbye for ever, dear Micheline.

Daddy didn't come to get her. As with the black girl, a dark limousine and a driver arrived. He put her suitcases in the boot, handed her her beautycase, opened the door for her. And off went Micheline like the others. The Scandinavians were the first to go, like their sun that sets soon after midday. Silent and pink they slipped away. Then it was Marion's turn. Again a dark car, the door opened for her. She rolled down the window and didn't deign to give me so much as a glance. Every time someone went, Frau Hofstetter came down into the yard, was dignified with the drivers, and a little disappointed that the gentlemen fathers hadn't come. She too gave her boarders a last kiss and they did a slight curtsey. My room-mate, the German, was taken away by her father in person in a black Mercedes. We had said goodbye in our room, a doltish goodbye, a brushing of cheeks. Goodbye, you're another person I shall never see again. The limousines grow scarcer. The rooms are empty, the windows abandoned to the landscape, the beds unmade, the soap bars still damp, covered in suds.

I'm the last. The gym, tennis and geography master takes me to the station. I've said goodbye to Frau Hofstetter, Herr Hofstetter; the marks on my report are modest. The Italian girl is leaving, she's tall, erect, has thick lips. Her father is the spitting image, the same thick lips, same thin nose, shortsighted, as if the eyes weren't there. He's wearing a dark striped suit. He tries to kiss Frau Hofstetter's hand, a clumsy proffering of lips. Walking between mother and father, the latter carrying the bags, with flat shoes and raven hair, the Italian girl heads for a taxi. Father and daughter with the heels of their socks threadbare. The shoes are new. They're a little confused, a little contrite, worried for that only daughter, the big strapping girl is so tall and her chin disappears when her mouth mimes a conversation. Heaven knows where they'll send her next year. A Swiss school is a reference for them.

Some time later I saw photographs of a young woman not unlike her: standing up, as if hanging. And aren't they our forerunners too somehow, these anonymous people we find in photographs? At least for those of us who spent our best years as boarders. We find our sisters in their faces. A strange familiarity binds us together, a cult of the dead. All those girls we knew have infiltrated our minds, become a tribe; and they come back to us in a sort of posthumous flowering. Perched like stylites on our brows, sleeping in a row of beds. I see my little companions from when I was eight years old, in bright white sheets, with their smiles, their lowered eyelids; their gaze has slipped away. We shared our beds with them. In prisons too, the prisoners don't forget their cellmates. They are faces that both fed and devoured our brains, our eyes. There is no time, at that time. Childhood is ancient.

From St. Gallen I took the train to Zurich, first class. Herr Dr., my father, was waiting on the platform. He lifted his hat. We go home. To a hotel. It's almost summer. At Easter there was the same blue sky, and the cock on the spire of a protestant church. There is something immobile here. '*Bist du zufrieden?*'

'*Ja, mein Vater.*' Are you happy? Yes, Father mine. Something immobile about the things we say too.

A year later I heard that Frau Hofstetter and her husband had died in a car accident. In the Appenzell. They were killed outright. And a son with them. They were the first of our teachers to die. But then our teachers are generally blessed with longevity.

They live a balanced life, for the most part in areas with a good climate, and I can't imagine that our education requires too much effort on their part. Maybe they, like the Hofstetters, will have experienced the occasional crush on a pupil. It is not unbecoming for a member of staff to take a fancy to a girl. It would be almost unthinkable that after years and years of self-denial and conscious satisfaction a Frau Hofstetter should not have felt a little unselfish love for one young lady at the expense of the others. Our teachers are certainly not without their sourness, a sourness to be found on the surface of their skin and in the tone of their voice, a sourness, one might be so bold as to say, directed at humanity in general. It is perhaps thanks to this sourness that for the most part these teachers of ours are good teachers.

When she went down to the village of Teufen, or when she took us to a concert in St. Gallen, Frau Hofstetter had a worried, rather dark look about her, in the foyer, amongst the crowd. She was too hot and the heat flushed her cheeks. Beneath her nose, a shiny wrinkle. Certainly she wasn't free to appreciate the concert, she had to look after the girls.

The world she came from, indeed that we all come from, the world beyond the sign *Töchterinstitut* written on the wall, didn't seem to be a friend to her. Even in the best of circumstances Frau Hofstetter always feared the worst. That evening in St. Gallen, for example, there was a terrible thunderstorm. The sky turned on us. The hailstones bounced on the street and we were obliged to wait. These atmospheric convulsions were great fun for us, they kept us out longer. Frau Hofstetter, with the impassivity of the condemned, scanned the horizon, the unknown land, whence at any moment catastrophe might strike.

We were malleable, she moulded us. But how could her gaze keep away a thunderstorm, a storm that perhaps had meant to play a trick on her? The teachers of this world, or at least those we knew, don't have a double life. During the year they teach, then they rest. They never venture out into the world. We don't miss our teachers. Perhaps sometimes we respected them too much, but that is part and parcel of the education we had, and if I kissed *Mère préfète's* hand every evening, without ever once protesting, it was because, quite apart from the rules, I took pleasure in it. The pleasure that comes from obedience. Order and submission, you can never know what fruits they will bear in adulthood. You might become a criminal or, by attrition, a normal conventional person. But one way or another we have been branded, especially those girls who spent from seven to ten years in boarding schools. I don't know what has become of us, I've heard nothing of the others. It's as if they were dead. Just one of them I looked for everywhere, her, Frédérique, because she goes on ahead of me. And I never stopped expecting a letter from her. She is not one of the dead. I was sure I wouldn't see her again, and that partly thanks to our education, which taught us to renounce the good things in life, to fear good news.

My education was still not complete. After the school on the island where being happy was the first rule, a last college smoothed out my seventeen years. A domestic management school. As ever the orders came from Brazil: I was to learn to keep house, to cook, to bake cakes. I had already learnt a bit of embroidery, at eight. It was now expected that I prepare myself to become a housewife. They found a school near a lake, Lake Zug, renowned for its cherry flans.

I had a nice room all to myself and four windows. It was a religious college. For once I spoke to the mother superior without pretending to be submissive and briefly explained my aversion to the training I was being offered. I didn't want to keep house, nor, I dared to tell her, did I want to be a wife. Over the idyll of my education resentment was dawning. Resentment towards that idyll, towards nature, the lakes, the floral compositions. The mother superior listened. I remember neither her face nor her body. '*Ich verstehe*,' she said. 'I understand.' And she left me in peace.

I read all day, I took walks, I went round the lake, and the other young ladies were in the kitchen learning. I spoke to no one; of the girls, like the mother superior, I recall no faces, no bodies. The one thing I remember with some precision is the geometry of my room. As far as Brazil was concerned, my education was complete. She, maman, had planned out my life, and my life had obediently followed her plan. I was finally free.

I received an invitation from Micheline to go to her eighteenth-birthday ball. I danced with her father. All fifteen girls from the Bausler Institut danced with Daddy. And Daddy flirted with them. Hadn't Micheline promised he would? There are promises which come true. Not just forebodings. Micheline was radiant. She put her eighteen years behind her that night.

The orchestra, the young people, the taffeta, the congratulations – you draw closer to old age. To the nightmares of promises. Hurry up, Micheline. Her father was tired. A well-preserved man, he'd been dancing with us for hours. And we who wanted to see this father, we who had old fathers and who suspected our parents of making orphans of us on purpose, spun in his arms, detesting this fun, this keeping of promises.

Micheline's dress was lace and silk and seemed to have been cut from time itself, so well suited was it for the ball and, Micheline fantasised, for her death bed. After dancing, she walked among the tables arm in arm with Daddy. Who was a fetish, with tanned skin and high cheekbones. Frédérique did not come to the party. I neither looked for her nor tried to think of her. What are the girls thinking of? At least half are nostalgic for death, and for a temple, and for all those clothes.

Another guest came in from the park. In a tight-fitting black dress, blacker than her hair, slim waist tied with a ribbon, back straight as an officer's. She had only just got off the boat. Her eyes were violet, like painted wax. She came at a measured pace, on high heels, trailing a shawl of black velvet that seemed alive. On her wrists were two black enamelled bracelets. Her smile didn't fade. She darkened our pastel-coloured dresses, which were roomy and tame. She looked like a widow. You could just sense her breasts and her determination. It was Marion. We stopped dancing. We gathered round her. Everybody touched her. Micheline bent forward to pick up the shawl that had fallen to the floor. At once a heel stopped her. 'Leave it there.' Imperious and cold. Now Marion is kissing her friend. She hugs her tight to herself in front of everyone. 'I'm sorry if I'm in black. My parents died in a plane crash. But it would take more than that to keep me away from Micheline's dance.'

I saw Frédérique again. By chance. At night. She looked like a ghost almost. Her head was hooded, hands in her pockets. She greeted me, calling me by name, and it was as though her voice were reaching me from far away. She had been at the Cinémateque too. We had never spoken of films at the Bausler Institut. Until now I had hardly ever been in a cinema. I wasn't allowed. There wasn't much I was allowed to do during my holidays from school. The summer before the orders had been: holidays by the sea. I hated the light and fell ill.

Hence if I had been allowed to choose, I would have proposed a dark place. And cinemas are dark places. After my illness they were the first place I went to. On the screen I saw everything I had missed. My first friends were friends from the cinema, the unknown viewers who bowed their heads, overcome by sleep and drowsiness, tramps. They sleep in tidy hedges. Their fingers are gloved in thick wool and lie still. Nervous ticks twitch their knees or necks. They wake. They'll come back tomorrow. To the same place. Some meet late in the evening. Pale navigators on the brink of life, of Hades.

I grabbed her arm, I was afraid she might disappear. Meek and sarcastic, Frédérique let me. Without taking her hands from her pockets. She had seen me getting rid of a boy, like a moneylender hiding cash. I pretended to be alone. Years later the boy was stabbed to death in a hotel room in Cairo. He had blond hair, round, boring cheeks with no hollows for the eyes, his hair just beginning to thin.

We walked without stopping. Apparently aimlessly. I had found her. It was her. She had been the most disciplined, respectful, ordered, perfect girl, it almost made your flesh creep. Where was she going? I followed her. She could even tidy the shelves of the void. '*Tu viens chez moi*,' she said. The gardens outside the Louvre were ice, the city the colour of ash, all the signs of commercial empires, clothing stores, funeral parlours and pastry shops, seemed blurred. Having walked by shop windows, mirrors and gates – and it was cold – she pushed a heavy door. Barely open, it closed with a bang. We climbed the stairs. I followed her footsteps. The walls seemed high. She said it was a block with nothing but offices. No one was there at night. At the top of the stairs she opened a wooden door that led to a corridor.

In the corridor was a small washbasin. And toilets. We went on down the long narrow corridor. It seemed we must be a long way from where we'd started, the entrance from the street. Then we stopped in front of another door and she gestured for me to go in.

I found myself in a room carved out of nothing. I felt the icy cold. It's a rectangle, a window at the far end, yellowing walls. '*J'habite ici.*' I was standing. She picked up a saucepan, poured in some alcohol and lit it. We stood watching the fire on the ground, the struggle, then death throes of the last darting flames. She told me she had seen some cockfights in Andalusia. '*La chaleur ne dure pas longtemps.*' And she had something Spanish about her, something ancient, something ecclesiastic. The blaze of heat died and the cold of the mountain tops and the glaciers swept down.

A bulb hung from the ceiling. She offered me the only seat. Under the bulb. She picked up a gnawed candle (was she living on wax?) and lit it with a match. The wick was buried. Her eyes, which took no light from the trembling flame, were bright, calm beneath, lacquered, alien. Her face was partly hidden by her hood, it could have been a veil of marble wrapped around her. Her beauty hadn't left her. Nor her determination. She looked at me with irony, challenge almost.

I thought of this destitution of hers as some spiritual or aesthetic exercise. Only an aesthete can give up everything. I wasn't surprised so much by her poverty as by her grandeur. That room was a concept. Though of what I didn't know. Once again she had gone beyond me. I tried to understand. She sat on a couch, on a bed that could have been made of stone, it didn't give, the way she didn't give. I looked around at all four walls, into the corners. The room was almost entirely in shadow. My eyes went from her face to the void. She was calm. Something very banal came to mind: we hadn't been educated to live like this. I was full of admiration. I felt cold. I put my woollen gloves back on and twisted my scarf a couple more times round my neck.

Frédérique was about twenty now. She dressed as she always had. A dark zinc grey over her body, narrow hips, long neck. The jugular was pulsing. She had pushed pack her hood. The pale oval of her face, legs crossed. The perfection of school days had taken up residence in this room of hers. A cynical expression crossed her face, her eyelids trembled. Then she was as before. Calm. Mocking. '*As tu froid?*' '*Pas tellement.*' She had no more alcohol to warm us. She lives, I thought, as if she were in a grave.

The cold bit into the bones, it was pure highland air. But I was beginning to get used to it. I took off scarf and gloves. Perhaps, with a little more practice, I would see a waterfall like a snake coming down from the wall, and a midnight sun. I struggled to open a window. She came across to me and we looked at the sky, arms folded. I thought of the toilets in the corridor. Were they abandoned or was someone using them? She didn't know, she only came at night, there wasn't anyone in the building at night.

Sometimes while she was speaking she would break off. '*Je cause avec eux.*' And she saw them. They came to see her. Sometimes they sat where I was sitting now. She laughed, like a bird in the night, shrill and sharp. So Frédérique speaks with the dead. I was the only 'living' person who had come to this room. Will I see you again? I asked. The new day was dawning, a cardboard dawn. I could come when I wanted. I wanted to come this very evening, and the next day, every day. She smiled, calm. After that night I couldn't find her again. I don't remember how I got out of her room, nor the corridor, nor the stairs. The stones and walls closed up behind me. In the room, when night began to grow pale, the shadows gathered in a tangle on the floor, until the light poured in. The only thing missing there was a rope.

Some years later, Frédérique tried to burn down her house in Geneva, the curtains, the paintings and her mother. Her mother was reading in the lounge.

That was when I got to know Madame. She was around sixty, everything about her was soft: her complexion, her skin, her dress, her calves, the pink, vulnerable fattiness of her chin. Her eyes were a faded blue, serene and incorruptible as they weighed me up, then propelled me toward the lounge. Immaculate white curtains covered the windows, the lace was like icing sugar. Madame sits down. I'm still on my feet. I'm overtaken by a general feeling of indecision. I'd like to get out of here. I do as Madame does and sit down. A number of portraits hang on the walls, immersed in shadow and sleep.

The sun was shining brightly over Geneva; Madame had commanded dusk. The filtered light brought out the surfaces of things, the fervourless indolence of cushions and upholstery. On an oval table stood a clouded silver teapot and some teacups. A few petits fours had been scattered on a dish. White napkins bearing the initials of the dead. Perhaps the initials of those in the portraits, watching from lidless eyes. On another round table, where centuries, or hours before someone had leaned an elbow, a vase proffered a floral composition, Flemish. A butterfly would have been too extravagant, it would have interfered with the meditation of the petals. No breath of wind was to spoil their ephemeral blaze.

The air was heavy, an atmosphere of drowsy convalescence. The stillness of a desk in a corner, its stack of little drawers, ivory knobs, conjured up an invisible scribe with neither pen nor paper, dictating his letters to no one. Madame's hands had composed the objects, both living and dead. The living included herself, the rings on her finger, wedding rings, a golden charnel house, oases of widowhood and betrothal.

Madame poured the tea, she poured slowly until the cups were half full, offered the petits fours. '*Je vous en prie*, dear.' She brought the cup to her lips, concentrated on some thought that remained unformulated, suspended in the air. On the walls the faces of the portraits seemed to grow animated, twitched nervously in their cracks. She smiled at me, I smiled at her. So, I was a friend of her daughter's, her daughter who had no friends. She was pleased to meet me, she said sweetly, politely. It was almost convincing; I was grateful for that almost, that faint uncertainty attenuating every brusque opposition between true and false. Her eyes cloaked me in an almost girlish gaze, an innocent gaze. They were a girl's eyes, they wouldn't be disturbed, or a doll's, without idiocy or amazement. A curdled paradise, the Genevan lake-blue irises streaked. Madame seems to be happy. With extraordinary sweetness she asks me what hotel I'm staying in. 'At the Hôtel de Russie.' 'It's falling to pieces,' she said. 'They'll knock it down,' she added confidently.

The rooms, I went on, are large and spacious, real *salons*, I said with emphasis (as though to protect the hotel from destruction). Yes, she knew, but in bad repair. Stubbornly, but with the same sweetness, she asked after my dear parents. And if they were Protestants. I mentioned to Madame that we had already met once. Sweetly, she seemed not to remember. I insisted: it was the day she had come to get Frédérique at the school. And I went with you, I said, to the station. Now Madame remembered, '*une jeune fille triste*', a charitable smile trembled her chin. She didn't speak about times past, but about the weather, the heat and humidity. She was well informed about matters meteorological. Her calm and sweetness were sumptuous, a thick velvet. And durable too, they could have been used to improve doors and windows. I took some more petits fours, she apologised for not having offered them twice. I counted them, there were five or six left on the plate. I decided to finish them. My mind went back over all the mamans I had known from my school. I felt faintly repulsed. For no reason. I saw them in the drawing rooms where we would meet them, in their tailleurs, moving their lips.

Some drawing rooms, especially those in the religious schools, have something sinister and conspiratorial about them. In my first school, run by nuns, when I was eight, we were all obsessed by 'spies', a word that brought cosmic resonance to tale-telling. That was what I was thinking of when Madame poured the now lukewarm tea into our cups.

Frédérique hadn't said a word. Her silence had no weight to it. It was lifeless, alien. All at once she started. Until now she had been sitting in the middle of a sofa, sitting as if about to get up and go, her bust leaning slightly forward. She let out a rasping sigh, then another. Her breath seemed to leave her chest as if with an echo, a rumbling, a second voice. Madame kept her cup in her hand, she remarked that in the Appenzell the men went to vote with their swords while the women watched from the window; and Madame turned toward the window, but I realised she was looking at her daughter. She had found a reason for looking at her. Madame went back to the weather. The acrid exuberance of the *vanitas* gave off a greenhouse perfume. Madame stroked a petal. Frédérique lifted her chest with sudden violence to take a breath. Her chest rose and fell, the rhythm was constant now, as if being gripped by spasms. Her breath whistled. For the first time I caught a dullness in her eyes, an expression of disorientation, a haze.

'My daughter', Madame whispered, showing me to the lift, 'tried to burn me.' She said it so sweetly it sounded like a regret. She opened the lift door. Inside was a mirror and a bench. '*Elle n'est pas responsable.*' And in the mirror I saw her crystalline eyes, tearful with trust, concise as an epitaph. You try to believe that, my dear. I can show myself out. She pressed the button. 'This is quite a trip for me. I keep guard. I almost never leave the house. You know what I mean, don't you?' After you. I made a gesture to let her go out first. She pushed me toward the door. Finally she said goodbye, thanking me for my visit, radiant because she had met her daughter's friend. The door closed.

It was a clear, grim day. The lake lapped in the wind. By the parapet an Asian delegation was getting into line. Silver hoops dangled from a fountain as if from a gallows. Frédérique had arranged to meet me in a café. I was early. The minutes passed slowly. I asked for a glass of Ovaltine. I had nothing to think about. The hands of the clock were still. A streaked leaf and a white butterfly courted each other. The leaf fluttered, mindful of the sap it once had, and the butterfly followed it, like a messenger. Idyll and death in a graceful whirling.

The table was marble. I asked for another glass of Ovaltine. I must find something to think about to pass the time. I thought of the railway stations, Teufen, Staz, Rigi, Wengen. I had taken swimming lessons in a pool and my father, in winter clothes, would sit in the shade, rejecting the summer sun. A wrong sun shone on our summers, a leaden sun pierced our twilight, a light of woods and marshes, a light that didn't come from above but seeped out from the toadstools and poisoned berries, the damp soil. We were walking toward that dark light, an oasis of walled-in peace. Father and daughter, hand in hand, like an old married couple. He pointed and told me the names of the mountains. In the hotel a metallic light lay across the tables, the croissants, the silverware. It was breakfast. A large window looked out on Cervino, the sun, the regeneration of the world. At the next table a woman and her three daughters caught our attention. Their bulging foreheads generated an air of such happiness. They were born well, I thought, they were born happy. The woman and the little girls displayed an almost stubborn happiness, demonically relaxed features.

'You see,' I said to my father, '*wie glücklich sie sind.*' (Perhaps he thought it was me was happy, he was distracted.) That whole day I was haunted by the vision of their sumptuously laid table and their happiness. The one on the right was the youngest, I thought; she had the smallest head, the narrowest forehead, the least obvious eyes. Thin nostrils. She wore her hair like the eldest, a fierce parting in the middle, frivolous in its fierceness. During our walk, the happiness that frolicked with the woman and her daughters presented itself in sharp contrast to my father and myself, alone every year, obstinately alone, a little sour, set in our ways, nervous if, as happens in hotels, someone trying to please should sit at our table. We say good morning to the people sitting at the next table. We would say goodbye when we got up to go. We always finished first.

We read in the lobby, the sound of a band drifted over from the lounge. Elderly couples danced the waltz, the fox-trot, the men taking long steps, keeping time. The Swiss have always had rhythm in their blood. When the French were there and they were celebrating the guillotine, the Swiss danced with them, raising their knees and showing the soles of their shoes.

The following day the hotel was unable to keep it a secret: the youngest daughter, she was my age, had hung herself in her room from the curtain with its pattern of flowers and leaves. So as not to disturb the guests things were done discreetly and we didn't see the corpse. Appearances did not violate the natural order of things.

It's true that a suicide is not in the natural order of things. But what's the difference? In the room the curtain was drawn to again. I thought of winter, in hotels. The icicles weeping on the branches outside, they would melt in spring. I never saw them melting.

And Frédérique arrives. She sits down. Her face is close to mine. We look at each other. Is it sorcery that brings lovers together? We joke. She smiles. It's our last meeting. 'What did you do with that doll?' 'What doll?' She looked me straight in the eyes. She has always kept hers; and she seemed to be saying that she kept it on her, in a pocket. The doll, she explained patiently, that the school gave us, the St. Gallen doll, with its costume and cap. 'Oh, I threw mine away as soon as I got it,' I said. 'No, you didn't, you'd better look for it, you must have left it somewhere. You'll find it, you'll see, I'm sure you didn't throw it away.' And it's almost as if she were reproaching me. She's like a saint, there's still a glimmer of ferocity in her eyes, a moment before she turns meek. She was sure I couldn't have thrown away that doll. It would have been a terrible thing to do. She was still insisting on being the most disciplined of us all, the most obedient. And she even seemed to be reproaching me for not having remembered that stuffed toy with its *Tracht* and painted eyes. I take her hand. The hand that wrote at school, in Teufen. And I copied her handwriting. She wants an example. I write her name on a scrap of paper. She who copies becomes the artifice. Goodbye, Frédérique. It's she who writes the word *adieu*. That small philistine sound I heard in Teufen is repeated now, turned on its head, it flattens out, it surrenders, it becomes part of the language of the dead.

Twenty years later she wrote me a letter. Her mother had left her something to live on. But she had had enough of the mental home, if she went on staying there, she'd be on her way to the cemetery.

I'm standing in front of the school building. Two women are sitting on a bench. I greet them with a nod. They don't respond. I open the door. A woman sitting behind a table. Another standing. She asks me what I want. I ask about the school. I say the name. She's never heard of it. Here in Teufen, *sind Sie sicher*? She looks at me with mean, enquiring eyes. Of course I'm sure. I lived here. For a moment my answer seems trivial. She advises me to go to St. Gallen. There are a lot of schools there. I repeat the name of the school. I am mistaken she says. I apologise. This, she says, is a home for the blind. That's what it is now. A home for the blind.